To asher

Merry Christmas!

Nancy Claus
2009

1917/1995

Santa's Secret

written by
Nancy Claus

illustrated by
Steve Ferchaud

CYPRESS
BAY
PUBLISHING

Cypress Bay Publishing • Woodbridge, CA
www.CypressBayPublishing.com

Dec. 22

My Goodness! Only 3 days before Christmas, and there is still a lot to do. Santa and the elves are working day and night. I wish there was something I could do to help...There is!!! I'll make a quick trip to the market to buy Santa some hot chocolate, a pair of warm new mittens, and a new sweater for his trip. After all, I wouldn't want Santa to catch cold!

"Now where did I
leave my boots?

"In the closet?
No."

"Under the bed? No."

"Behind the door? No."

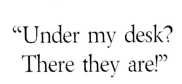

"Under my desk?
There they are!"

"Ryan, Brady, I need you to come with me. We have some shopping to do for Santa's trip."

"Okay, Mrs. Claus. We're coming.
Let's not forget the reindeer.
They need lots of carrots."

"I'll drop you two off at the market. After we finish our errands, we'll meet at the Polar Burger — your favorite place to eat."

"Okay, Mrs. Claus, but we want to be home early."

"Why?"

"Uhh, no reason, Mrs. Claus," says Ryan.

"Boy, that was close! If Mrs. Claus found out about Santa's secret, he'd be very disappointed. We can't give away his surprise."

"Are you ready for lunch, Ryan?
How about you, Brady? I'm very hungry."

"We're ready, Mrs. Claus."

"Brady, why are you eating so fast? And you, Ryan?
You must be very hungry!

"Not really, Mrs. Claus," Ryan manages to say
between giggles.

"I sure wish I knew what you two were up to!
You've been acting silly all day."

"Oh, Mrs. Claus, we're just excited."

"Excited? Excited about what?"

"Uhh, err…Nothing, Mrs. Claus," Ryan and Brady both cover their mouths to keep from giggling.

"Well, I can see you're not going to tell me your secret. We had better get back to the North Pole so I can help Santa."

"Oh, my goodness. Where is all that smoke coming from? And why is it pink? Why are there so many hearts? I had better go find Santa!"

"Santa?"

"Santa … Santa!"

"Santa, what have you done? Why did you turn everything into hearts?"

"Ho, ho, ho, Mrs. Claus. Did you forget what day it is? It's your birthday."

"No, I didn't forget, but everyone is so busy getting ready for Christmas Eve that I didn't think anyone would remember."

"Oh, Mrs. Claus. You make my heart so happy.
You think of everyone but yourself. I love you so much.
I have something I want you to see in my workshop.
Close your eyes and hold my hand."

"So this was the secret you two were
keeping from me."

"Mrs. Claus, it was so hard keeping Santa's secret
from you."

"Santa, this is the best surprise party I've ever been to.
I love the games, the songs, and dancing with you.
Thank you!"

"Oh, but there's more, Mrs. Claus …"

With the horns sounding, everyone sang,

"Your special day is finally here.
The one you've waited for all year.
We'll have cake and ice cream, too,
and more surprises just for you!"

"Santa, thank you for making my birthday
   so special. I love you very much!"

Dear Diary,
I still can't believe I didn't know anything about Santa's big surprise. It was so much fun! I still can't stop smiling.
Good Night.

This story is dedicated to
my Mom and Dad.
–Nancy Claus

Published by Cypress Bay Publishing
PO Box 984
Woodbridge, CA 95258-0984
www.cypressbaypublishing.com

Illustrations by Steve Ferchaud
Cover and interior design © TLC Graphics, www.TLCGraphics.com

SUMMARY: Santa gives Mrs. Claus a surprise birthday party.

First U.S. edition 2004

Printed in Hong Kong

ISBN 0-9746747-3-7
LCCN 2004094002